GYM, TANNING, LAUNDRY

THE OFFICIAL JERSEY SHORE QUOTE BOOK

GALLERY BOOKS

MTV BOOKS

New York   London   Toronto   Sydney

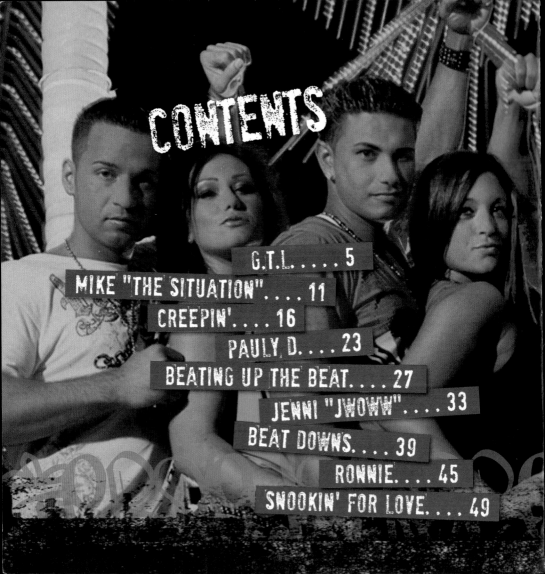

CONTENTS

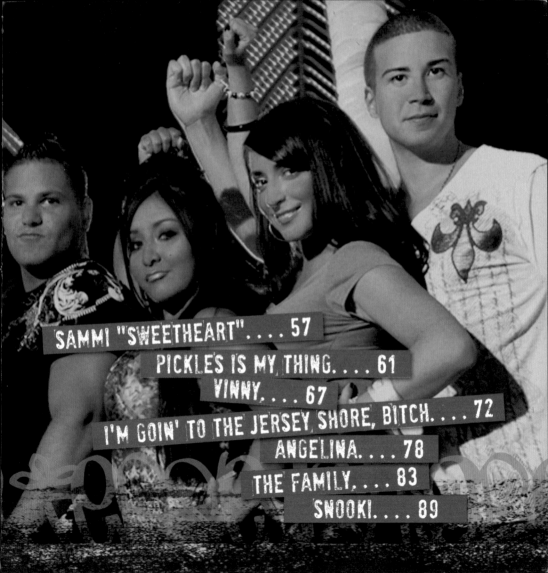

G.T.L.

G.T.L. BABY. GYM. TANNING. LAUNDRY.

—MIKE "THE SITUATION"

YOU GOT TO GO TO THE GYM THE WHOLE WEEK. You have to have a little color if you didn't go to the beach. And then the last thing that you need to take care of is the outfit. . . . Now, if the outfit's not looking good then the whole package is off. And if you feel off, you're not gonna have a good night. So how do you get the best results? G.T.L. baby. Gym, Tanning, Laundry. Because if everything's put together and you feel great, you look great: awesome night. —Mike "The Situation"

I WAIT 'TIL THE LAST MINUTE TO GO SHAVE. I wait 'til the last minute to put the shirt on. 'Cause it feels fresh. These are rules to live by. Shave last minute, haircut the day of, maybe some tanning and the gym. You gotta get the Guido handbook. —Mike "The Situation"

Dude, I got a f*ckin' tanning bed in my place, that's how serious I am about being a Guido and living up to that lifestyle. —Pauly D

I DON'T FOLLOW THOSE RULES AT ALL. I could see if it was like Basketball, Pool, Beach. Gym, Tanning, Laundry? Those aren't fun things at all. —Vinny

YOU GOTTA STAY FRESH-TO-DEATH—fresh outfit, fresh haircut, fresh tan, just stay fresh. —Pauly D

YOU BETTER BE HITTIN' THE GYM. And if you're not hittin' the gym for like an hour or so, you know you may have a problem. Okay, 'cause I'm at the gym for, like, an hour-and-a-half. You know, workin' on my fitness. —Mike "The Situation"

LET'S GO TANNING. If we got a little time, maybe we'll go to the gym and then get ready for tonight. You need that color—a little touch up on the paint job. —Mike "The Situation"

GUYS WITH THE BLOWOUTS AND THE FAKE TANS and guys that wear lip-gloss and makeup, those aren't Guidos, those are retards. —Vinny

A GUIDETTE IS SOMEBODY WHO KNOWS HOW TO CLUB IT UP, takes really good care of themselves, has pretty hair, cakes on makeup, has tanned skin, wears the hottest heels. They know how to own it and rock it. —Sammi

I love being a Guidette. —Snooki

IN A WEIRD SNOOKERS WORLD, like, me and Snookers would make the best little Guidos and Guidettes. Little poofs and blowouts on our little kids. —Pauly D

8

I WAS BORN AND RAISED A GUIDO. IT'S JUST A LIFESTYLE. IT'S BEING ITALIAN. IT'S REPRESENTING, FAMILY, FRIENDS, TANNING, GEL, EVERYTHING.

—PAULY D

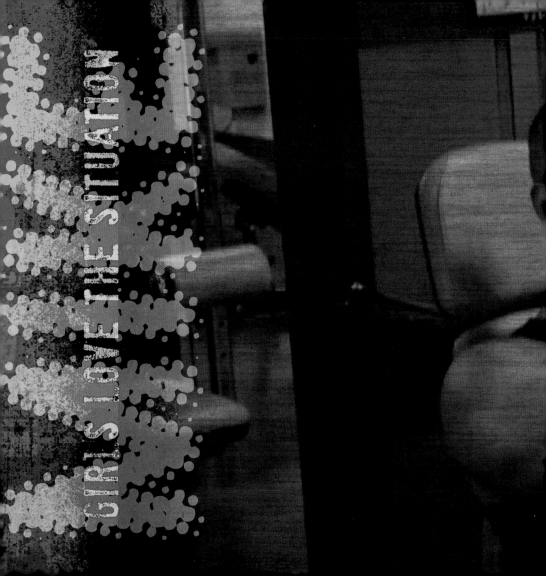

MIKE "THE SITUATION"

YOU CAN HATE ON ME ALL YOU WANT TO, BUT WHAT CAN YOU POSSIBLY SAY TO SOMEBODY THAT LOOKS LIKE RAMBO, PRETTY MUCH, WITH HIS SHIRT OFF.

I GOT GIRLS BACK HERE ALMOST EVERY NIGHT. There's not a time that I don't have girls comin' back. Girls love The Situation.

IF YOU WANT TO LOOK SOMEWHAT LIKE THE SITUATION, which is gonna be pretty hard, you need to get that protein in your diet.

EVERYBODY AT THE SHORE DEFINITELY KNOWS THE SITUATION. As far as I know, everybody loves The Situation, and if you don't love The Situation, I'm gonna make you love The Situation.

I MEAN THIS SITUATION IS GONNA BE INDESCRIBABLE, you can't even describe the situation that you're about to get into the situation.

> Mike would bang a Gatorade bottle if it had a pulse at this point. —Ronnie

MIKE CAN BE A NICE GUY. Like, he shows his good side, then he shows his jerk-off side. And that's what I like: a good guy and a jerk-off. It's all the same. —Snooki

SITUATION EXPECTS ME TO JUMP ON A GRENADE. But I'm not taking one for the team for Situation. Like, I learned a long time ago being wingman for Situation is not a good idea. —Pauly D

CREEPIN'

GOING FISHING

I'M HOOKING UP WITH MY GIRL. PAULY IS HOOKING UP WITH HIS GIRL. AND WE'RE GOING TO HAVE SEX. THAT'S THE SITUATION.
—MIKE "THE SITUATION"

All the girls are like fish and so we throw out a line and see if we can sink it. —Pauly D

PAULY AND MIKE ARE ALWAYS LOOKING FOR GIRLS, you know what I mean? I think they're going fishing tonight. They'll probably scrape something off the boardwalk. —Ronnie

WHEN I GO INTO THE CLUB I HAVE A GAME PLAN. I don't want to waste my time and take home a girl that just wants to hang out. I just wanna get to the business . . . so you line it up and then you move on . . . and at the end of the night you see who you end up with. —Pauly D

THERE IS DEFINITELY A NUMBERS GAME WHEN IT COMES TO GIRLS. Let's just say, you know, ten girls have slipped you their number within that particular week. There is a possibility that, like, five or six may not answer. Somebody may pick up, but they're busy. . . . Well probably on three and four they're probably coming over and I'm gonna have to make a decision on which group of girls I want to come over. —Mike "The Situation"

WOMEN ARE DEFINITELY A GAME. It's like a business. . . . There's rules to it and, like, boys take care of boys. —Pauly D

BASICALLY, ONE OF THESE GIRLS WAS DEFINITELY MORE CUTER than the other and it happened to be my girl and Pauly D was with "the grenade." When you go into battle, you need to have some friends with you so that just in case a grenade gets thrown at you, one of your buddies takes it first. —Mike "The Situation"

THERE'S ONE HUGE GRENADE LAUNCHER, there's one grenade, and then there's, like, one cute one. —Mike "The Situation"

SHE WAS A BOMB, pretty much, and Pauly did not know the code to decipher the bomb.
—Mike "The Situation"

I WAS WILLING TO TAKE ONE FOR THE TEAM, just so my boy could get some. —Pauly D

I'LL ENTERTAIN A CHICK SO MY BOY CAN GET SOME ASS and then once it gets to a certain point . . . if it's taking too long . . . It should be strictly business: Jacuzzi, bedroom, take care of business. —Pauly D

Pauly immediately fleed the scene and left me in arm's way.
—Mike "The Situation"

WHEN WE'RE OUT ON THE BATTLEFIELD, I'm like the first strike. . . . It's sort of like they send me out first, like the Navy SEALS. I get sent out and, like, a little reconnaissance, I bring girls back and then I share them with everybody else. —Mike "The Situation"

I WAS TAKIN' HEAVY FIRE and I didn't wear my bulletproof vest and I just don't know if I'm gonna make it. —Mike "The Situation"

That jerk-off just went to go creep. Wake me up if he doesn't come home with a bitch.
—Sammi

SNICKERS IS CRYING 'cause she got punched in the face and, like, The Situation is creepin'. How do you watch that girl get hit in her face and do nothing and like you still have the balls to creep. —Ronnie

LET'S GO, you got quarters so get outcha car. —Mike "The Situation"

THERE WAS THESE TWO GIRLS HE'S BEEN WORKING ON. He's like, "These girls will come home with us." I'm like "All right. That's cool, whatever." Got nothing else, right? They're the last. We might as well grab them. —Pauly D

THEY'RE COOL GIRLS. They're smart and everything, but they wanna hook up just as well. But I think it will take a couple of times seeing them to hook up. They're not, like, whores. —Pauly D

THERE ARE SOME GIRLS THAT ARE JUST GONNA COME HERE, strip off their clothes and jump in the Jacuzzi. Then there are girls that are respectful, that you have to just actually treat like girls, human beings. —Vinny

I'M NOT A BITCH.

PAULY D

THERE'S NO WAY I'M GOING TO JERSEY WITHOUT MY HAIR GEL, CAN'T LEAVE WITHOUT MY GEL.

MY HAIR'S WINDPROOF, waterproof, soccerproof, motorcycleproof . . . I'm not sure if my hair's bulletproof. I'm not willing to try that.

DON'T LET THE SPIKE HAIR FOOL YOU. Like, I'm not a bitch.

HIS DOUCHE BAG FRIEND said me and Pauly were bumping and grinding. —JWoww

HE SAID, "The tool bag with the blowout." I don't know who the fuck else that could be. —Tommy (JWoww's boyfriend)

PAULY PULLED OUT HIS DJ EQUIPMENT. He's got the Italian thing on his equipment. Then he has another Italian flag on his book bag, another Italian flag on his laptop. He's the ultimate Guido. —Ronnie

IT'S MY TURN to prove to the Jersey Shore how I get down, like, on the 1s and 2s.

GIRLS LOVE A DJ, SO ONCE THEY SEE ME BEHIND THE WHEELS OF STEEL OVER THERE, DOING MY THING . . . WATCH OUT!

GET READY TO PARTY

BEATING UP THE BEAT

GET READY TO PARTY, GET OUT THERE,
GET FILTHY, CREEPY, AND WEIRD.
—RONNIE

SNOOKI'S STAYING AND I'M READY TO PARTY. I'm ready to meet sexy Guidos and I'm ready just to f*cking be single. —Snooki

THE RON-RON JUICE IS THE SH*T that gets the night going. I mean, whenever that sh*t comes out it's always a filthy night. —Ronnie

IT'S SATURDAY NIGHT. We're going to Headliners. I'm looking to have more of a classy night tonight. —Vinny

I'M SO EXCITED because I could actually, like, let loose and be my full self. —Snooki

THIS LITTLE SHRIMP THING is, like, bopping all around on the circle and, like, doing her thing. Doing backwards flips with her thong hanging out; her whole crotch is in the air. —Sammi

THAT GIRL CAN SHAKE IT. Drop it like it's hot, girl. —Mike "The Situation"

28

WE'RE BEATIN'-UP-THE-BEAT. That's what we say when we're doing our fist pump. First, we start off by banging the ground, we're banging it as the beat builds 'cause that beat's hittin' us so we're fightin' back, it's like we beat up that beat. —Pauly D

I FEEL THE BEAT, right. It might just so happen that my fist might just pump in the air. —Vinny

I HEAR THE MUSIC. I start fist pumpin'. I start pulling girls up on stage and it's like now . . . Vinny came out to play. —Vinny

I WASN'T, LIKE, SEXUAL . . . It f*cking was house music. —Snooki

F-COVE IS A SPOT WHERE ALL THE BOATS MEET UP and they all tie together and have this, like, huge party. Party hop from boat to boat to boat. It's like paradise on the water. —Pauly D

OUR BOAT IS CALLED FURGETABOWDIT. And right when I saw that, I was like, "Yo, this is our boat." —Snooki

29

IT'S A.C. BITCH.
WHAT HAPPENS IN A.C. STAYS IN A.C.
—SNOOKI

JENNI "JWOWW"

I AM LIKE A PRAYING MANTIS. AFTER I HAVE SEX WITH A GUY I WILL RIP THEIR HEADS OFF.

I HAVE A BAD HABIT of playing little emotional games with men. When they date me it's cool in the beginning, we do our thing in the first month, and then I send them on a rollercoaster ride to hell.

I GUESS I'M SINGLE. I don't know. If I am, we've got a problem on our hands 'cause I've been like f*ckin' Susie Homemaker over here. I've been, uh, a nun, a Catholic nun, for all I know.

I SEE A BUNCH OF, LIKE, GORILLA JUICEHEADS. Tall, completely jacked, steroids, like, multiple growth hormone. And that's, like, the type that I'm attracted to.

I WAS REALLY PUMPED 'cause, you know, like, nobody's seen what I'm capable of. If I'm gonna be single, I'll f*cking make everyone hate each other by the end of the night.

There are so many juiceheads out there. I'm like a kid in a candy shop.

IF HE DOESN'T WANT TO MAKE IT WORK, THEN IT'S NO-HOLDS. I'M JUST GONNA SHOW MY TRUE SIDE. MY TRUE, DIRTY, FILTHY F*CKING SIDE.

SHE JUST DOESN'T WANT TO FEEL LIKE A TRASH BAG because she has a boyfriend and she kissed me with the tongue. —Pauly D

JWOWW'S P*SSY must bring rainbows and pots of treasure. —Ronnie

IF JWOWW WAS MY GIRL, I would break up with her in a second. Your girl shouldn't be out there dancing like that, lifting up her skirt. And I already made out with her. —Pauly D

I would give her f*ckin' bubblegum. I would send her a picture of my d*ck and a pack of bubblegum and say "chew on this." —Ronnie

All of a sudden, Jenni starts coming at me. F*ckin' throwing out the wig, throwing out the fake nails.

—Mike "The Situation"

I THINK THE FACT THAT MIKE GOT PUNCHED in the face by Jenni is pretty funny. —Vinny

THE POWER THAT WAS BEHIND IT was some video game sh*t.

—Vinny (On JWoww's punch)

SHE GOT THROWN OUT OF THE CLUB like the piece of trash that she is.

—Mike "The Situation"

BEAT DOWNS

LIKE, DID I JUST GET HIT BY A GUY?
—SNOOKI

Please don't tell me I have missing teeth! —Snooki

THIS WAS JUST A REGULAR GIRL, like my sister or my friends, and you're, like, a grown ass guy and you punch her in the mouth? —Vinny

THAT KID IS NEVER GONNA BE ABLE TO F*CKING WALK this earth again 'cause he's known as punching a girl in the face. —Vinny

HE BETTER NOT HOPE I don't find out his name, bro. —Ronnie

THIS KID IS SO LUCKY the cops were there because I was about to barrel through cops, I was that heated. —Vinny

SOMEONE THREW A DRINK and then all of a sudden it was like World War III or something. —Pauly D

THIS ONE GIRL STARTS like charging me like a f*ckin' hippo. —Snooki

THROUGH THE SCUFFLE Snooks gets hit in the face, again. Poor girl . . . she needs to take some karate classes or somethin'. She needs self-defense. Somebody's got to teach her how to fight or duck. —Pauly D

I JUST FOUGHT TWO BITCHES that I don't even care about for my roommate that's a frickin' retard for bringing them back. —Snooki

GO HOME. You don't belong here. You don't even look Italian! —Sammi

I FELT BAD ABOUT SNICKERS getting hit by a couple linebackers. I necessarily didn't want to bring home any sort of zoo creatures whatsoever. I mean, these broads just probably smelled the food at the house. —Mike "The Situation"

My face is f*cked up again. —Snooki

HIS GIRLFRIEND STARTS SWINGING AT ME, scratches the side of my face. I didn't want to raise my hand to her, so, like, I just, like, kept backing up. But at the same time, this guy is trying to swing over his girlfriend, which is completely a bullsh*t move. —Ronnie

AT SEASIDE TROUBLE'S ALWAYS GONNA FIND YOU. I mean, I had to control the situation. And I end up spending the night in county for—not even the night, a few hours in county—for, you know, overreacting, I guess, like a degenerate that I'm not. —Ronnie

No man will ever touch me like that ever twice.
—Sammi

I would have tried to uppercut her, but at that point I had too many bouncers wrapped around me. I just wish for, like, three more seconds. I woulda done justice.
—JWoww

AND SHE WAS LIKE, "Yeah, I'm done with this sh*t. Like, you don't push a girl." And I understand where she's coming from 'cause I just got hit in the face by a guy. —Snooki

SHE CALLED SNICKERS FAT and that, like, triggered me. So I threw my drink in her face. —JWoww

I LOOK OVER AND I SEE, like, hair being pulled and all this sh*t. I'm like, "Oh my God, how do I get in?" —Snooki

RONNIE

MY ONLY RULE: NEVER FALL IN
LOVE AT THE JERSEY SHORE.
—RONNIE

I mean I'll break it down dancing. I love the beats. I got my creepy patent move.

(On his mom) **IT'S LIKE, RELAX,** you know what I mean? Like, just f*cking drink your mimosa, smoke another cigarette and f*cking take it easy.

ME AND SAM actually leave around, like, 4 o'clock. We've been here since 12 o'clock. Five hours is, like, enough.

I LIKE HER TO BE HONEST WITH YOU. At first I was all about "I'm not gonna sh*t where I sleep." But, I mean, for her I'll roll around in my sh*t all day. —Ronnie

We hold hands in front of you, we cuddle in front of you, we make out in front of you. Do I need to beat it in front of you, too? —Ronnie

THIS IS NO JOKE, how I feel about you. Like, you don't even understand that. —Sammi

LIKE, YOU'RE LEGIT my girl right now. —Ronnie

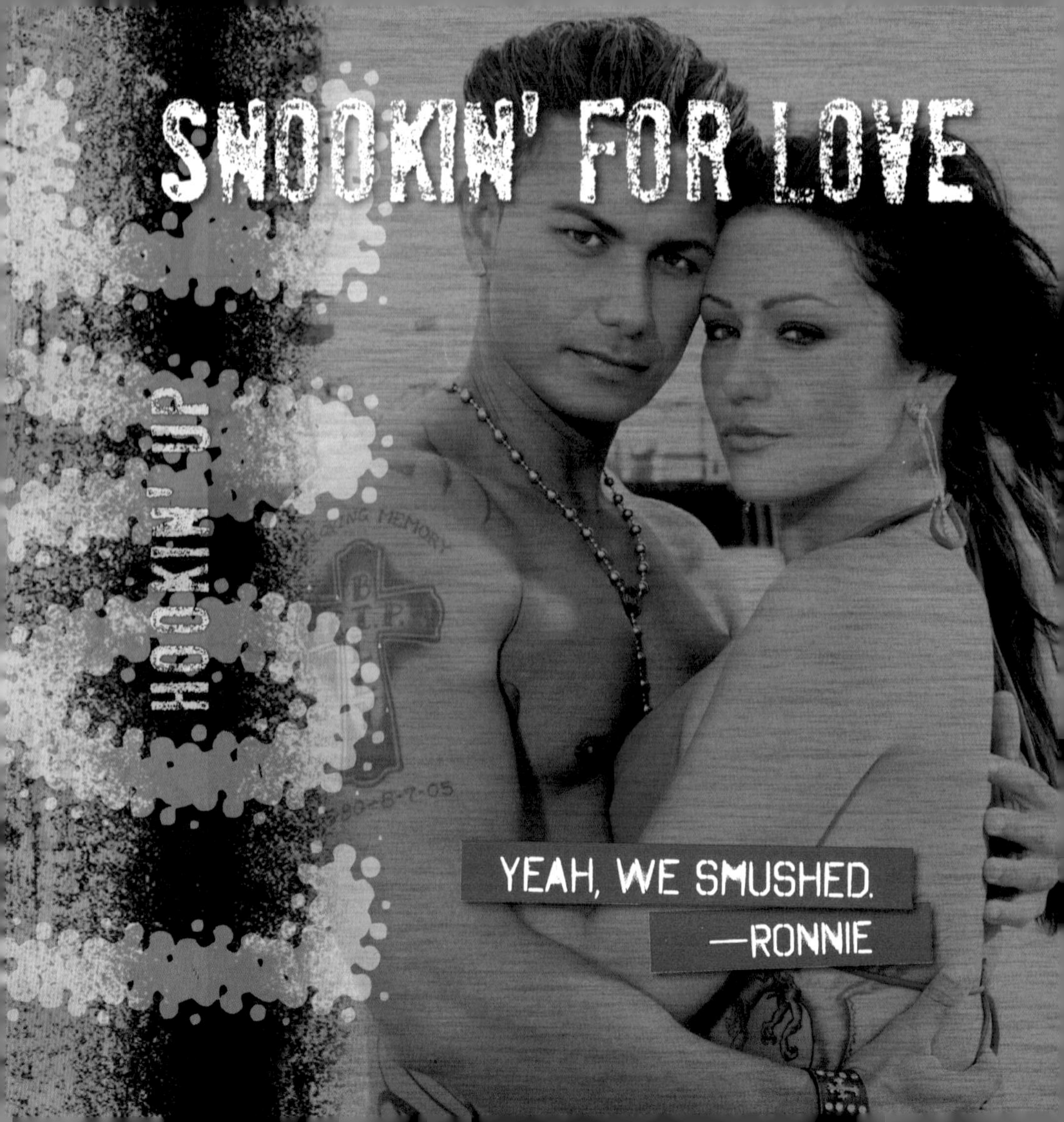
SNOOKIN' FOR LOVE
HOOKIN' UP
YEAH, WE SMUSHED.
—RONNIE

ANY RELATIONSHIP, IT'S THE SAME OLD THING. It's like, goo-goo ga-ga, like reach out for each other in the beginning. Then you get really comfortable and then sh*t goes down where you just can't even deal with each other anymore. —Sammi

MY IDEAL MAN WOULD BE ITALIAN, dark, muscles juicehead Guido. If I found that guy, I'd snatch him like that. —Snooki

STEPHANIE IS A GIRL I MET at Bamboo, and she's actually a pretty girl that I'm attracted to, to the point where I'd rather do sweet things for you instead of, you know, just come home and hook up. It's like a different situation. —Mike "The Situation"

A few days ago I told my boyfriend that I saw Pauly's piercing on his penis.
—JWoww

LIKE, I'D DEFINITELY HOOK UP WITH HIM. If sh*t happens, sh*t happens, you know. If one thing leads to another, I'm not gonna tell him to get off. —Snooki

I JUST MET THIS GIRL and she already stalks my whole life. —Pauly D

I'M LIKE, WHAT? What the hell is wrong with me? Like, I always pick the f*ckin' losers. —Snooki

I usually don't feel bad about taking someone's girl, per se, because that's the girl's fault.
—Vinny

I'M NOT TRYING TO MAKE YOU PLAY IT OUT. If I see you, physically on the dance floor with another girl, like, then forget you. —Sammi

I WAS TRYING to put you in the equation. Like, you, in the equation. —Ronnie

I'M SITTING HERE trying to convince you that I care. If I didn't, I'd just walk away and go find another creature outside. —Ronnie

GUYS ARE ALL THE SAME. I put money on it he brings home a bitch and gets with her tonight, on purpose. —Sammi

IF I WAS JUST GONNA GET SLOPPY, I should have just pounded out what's her name on Friday night. —Ronnie

I WILL SUCK YOUR BIG TOE right now. I don't give a sh*t.
—Ronnie

I PERSONALLY DON'T CARE what other people think. We're going out. Like, f*ck you. See you later. —Sammi

YES, I HAD SEX, LIKE HELLO, you're gonna have sex if you're into somebody. It's natural. —Sammi

I couldn't have sex with my girl, she had her period. I go to take her pants off—she wouldn't let me, no big deal. —Pauly D

SHE'S KISSING ME. Kissing on my neck, kissing on my chest. Her hands were going downstairs. —Pauly D

I JUST WANTED TO GO HOME and make out with my friend Mike. So I just tested him a little. I was like, "Listen, if you want to, like, go meet girls, whatever, you can go." He freakin' jumped out of the car like it was on f*ckin' fire. —Snooki

LIKE, THAT PISSES ME OFF. Like, right when I f*ckin' met a guy and I went to get his number and hang out with him, we had to leave. Just my luck. —Snooki

I HATE GUYS. I'm turning lesbian. I swear. —Snooki

THE SWEETEST BITCH

SAMMI "SWEETHEART"

I'M THE SWEETEST BITCH YOU'LL EVER MEET, BUT DO NOT F*CK WITH ME.

YOUR NUMBER ONE MISSION is to go out and find the hottest Guido and take him home.

IF YOU'RE NOT A GUIDO then you can get the f*ck outta my face.

LIKE WHEN I LEFT KARMA, I didn't even know what was going on in my head. Like, I'm gonna f*ckin' knock a bitch up.

I DEFINITELY WANNA LOOK GOOD FOR RONNIE'S PARENTS because this is the first time they're meeting me and, like, I want them to think like "Wow. That's her. She's really pretty," and whatever.

DON'T CALL 911, I think that's emergency.

With me and Sam, it's not a matter of if she wants to hook up with me; it's a matter of just when I decide.
—Mike "The Situation"

IT'S OBVIOUS that Sammi has a crush on me. It goes back to the days of prehistoric kindergarten. —Mike "The Situation"

THIS WHOLE THING IS WITH SAM, she wants nothing to do with you. I closed that deal a long time ago; I already got the title for that closing. —Ronnie

I WAS KINDA GETTING, LIKE, ANNOYED with Sammi because, like, the way she talks sometimes, like, she can be a real bitch and she doesn't even, like, realize it. —Snooki

PICKLES IS MY THING

SALUD

WE COORDINATED A FEAST
WHILE YOU WERE GETTING YOUR
NAIL AND YOUR HAIR DID TODAY.
—MIKE "THE SITUATION"

Girls are supposed to cook and the guys are supposed to eat, but Mikey did his thing. We had like peppas.
—Pauly D

SALUD, you big pimps. —Ronnie

GOOD JOB, YOU COOKED FOOD FOR EVERYONE. Have I ever asked you to cook me food? No. Do you do it? Yeah. —Sammi

EVERYBODY SHOULD TAKE EACH SIDE of my plate and walk it to the garbage. —Mike "The Situation"

I'M NOT TOUCHING ONE DISH, because I cooked a crazy meal and she's got the nerve to tell me to clean my plate. You know what? You are excluded from dinner then. From now on you are excluded from the surf 'n' turf night. You're excluded from ravioli night. You're excluded from chicken cutlet night. —Mike "The Situation"

IT'S FUNNY, 'cause he cooked, he cleaned. He did everything that my mother does. So he was the woman of the house. —Ronnie (On Mike)

I CAME HOME when they were putting in the lobsters, I was like "Yo, are those real?" That's disgusting. I'm a vet tech. Like, I save animals. I don't kill them. —Snooki

THAT'S WHY I DON'T EAT LOBSTER or anything like that 'cause they're alive when you kill it. —Snooki

VINNY'S MOM REMINDS ME OF MY GRANDMOTHER. Like, when she cooked, she never sits down . . . Like a true Italian woman. Like, you know, you want to please everyone else at the table and then when everyone's done eating, you clean up and then eat by yourself. So, you know, right from the bat, like, when she did that, I knew she was a great freakin' woman. —Snooki

SHE BROUGHT LIKE FOUR TRAYS OF FRICKIN' ZITI, the sauce, ya know, all this food. We got amazing cold cuts, loaves of bread. I'm like "Oh my God, it's f*ckin' Christmas." —Snooki

Don't make a joke outta grace.
—JWoww

I TRIED TO EAT but I couldn't get it in my freakin' mouth 'cause I'm disabled. —Snooki

I JUST WANT TO THANK GOD for everything that we have right now. Especially that Snickers is okay. —Vinny

YOU GET SOME FOOD. Feel better. Drink heavily. —JWoww

I'M FAT. I'm about to eat a sausage right now. F*CK YOU ALL!!! —Snooki

I LEFT THE CLUB EARLY because I didn't want to cheat on my boyfriend, and I felt like eating ham and drinkin' water. Ham. —JWoww

CAN I HAVE A ROLL **please?** —Snooki

DON'T WORRY, **you got a couple.** —Mike "The Situation"

SO WHAT I DECIDED TO DO WAS **get about, like,
three inches of grated cheese, add a little milk,
a little Supreme dressing , a tiny bit of mayo and
a little of Snickers's pickle juice all wrapped in one.
A little Hater-Ade.** —Mike "The Situation"

The boys, like, always stare at
me as I'm eating pickles 'cause
they're f*cking perverts.
—Snooki

NICE STATEN ISLAND KID

VINNY

I'M DEFINITELY A MAMA'S BOY. I DON'T TAKE ADVANTAGE OF HER, BUT AT THE SAME TIME SHE LIVES FOR TAKING CARE OF ME.

I DON'T THINK I'VE EVER HAD A GUEST BACK TO THE HOUSE, 'cause I'm not, like, a man whore, like, bringin' home girls like that.

I NEVER HAD GIRLS RUN UP TO ME like this before. And they were all hot. One of them, who I probably thought was one of the cutest girls there, like you know, fake boobs, nice butt, stomach showing, she said she was a model.

I don't give a f*ck. You're fat, you're ugly, you're 45-years-old, I'll dance with you.

That's what you get for putting a fat girl's ass in your face. That's how you get pinkeye.
—Ronnie

HE'S A NICE STATEN ISLAND KID. I didn't really mind hooking him up with my sister because the kid's harmless. And Vinny knows that I'm pretty much the man of the house and not to push it too far or I'm gonna, you know, throw him in my trunk. —Mike "The Situation"

VINNY'S FAMILY WALKS IN THE DOOR . . . Here comes the mom, here comes the sister, here comes, like, an aunt, a cousin, another cousin, then a little cousin, then another cousin. It's like they kept comin'. —Pauly D

I'M GOIN' TO THE JERSEY SHORE, BITCH

THREE GIRLS IN A JACUZZI

THE HOUSE IS F*CKIN' ATROCIOUS.
—RONNIE

OUR WHOLE SUMMER WAS JUST UNBELIEVABLE. Down here at the shore, one minute you got three girls in the Jacuzzi, the next minute somebody's in jail and you have to bail them out. That's what happens down at the shore. —Mike "The Situation"

I DID FEEL A LITTLE BAD ABOUT RONNIE getting arrested, because it went from having an awesome night—no fights—to Ronnie in jail. So it was just mad drama and that's just how sometimes the Shore goes. —Mike "The Situation"

I HAD, LIKE, THE BEST SUMMER OF MY LIFE. Girls on the rides, girls on the beach, girls in the house, hot tub. Girls after girls after girls. That's a ideal summer for anybody. —Pauly D

SHE'S LIKE, "EVERYBODY'S TALKING ABOUT MIKEY AND PAULY D. The Problem and The Situation. They're hooking up with everybody."
—Mike "The Situation"

All I wanna do is make a name for myself in Jersey.
—Pauly D

Yeah, this is a problem right now. We could possibly blow up right now.
—Mike "The Situation"

I TOLD PAULY TO START THE GRILL and he puts charcoal in a gas grill and then he asks me to light it. We were this close to pretty much blowing up the house. —Mike "The Situation"

NEXT THING YOU KNOW, the grill is legit burnt. Smoke, like flames. —Sammi

WHEN THERE WAS KNOCKIN' ON THE DOOR, I was like, this is either the police for me, this is either some lawyer, somebody's dad, somebody's brother. —Mike "The Situation"

THERE'S A WEIRD SMELL IN THE HOUSE. It kind of smells like old funk juice. It kind of has a pickley smell to it too. —Vinny

I RAN THE HOUSE . . . I did whatever I wanted, I took whatever I wanted and it was my world. —Mike "The Situation"

The friggin' duck phone.
—Snooki

NEW JERSEY NIGHTLIFE IS FUN. IT'S CRAZY. PEOPLE GRINDING ON EACH OTHER, DOGGING EACH OTHER OUT. IT'S A GOOD TIME.

—RONNIE

ANGELINA

MORE CLASSIER

I AM THE KIM KARDASHIAN
OF STATEN ISLAND, BABY.

I AM ALL NATURAL. I have real boobs. I have a nice fat ass. Look at this sh*t, I mean, come on, I'm hot.

HOW DO YOU GO IN A F*CKING JACUZZI with a thong and a bra? Wear a thong bikini, that's a little bit more classier if you're gonna wear anything at all.

I FEEL LIKE THIS JOB IS BENEATH ME. I'm a bartender. I do, like, great things.

I'M JUST, LIKE, YOU KNOW WHAT? I'm thinking about my boyfriend so much and I'm, like, I really don't want to work today.

YO, I WILL CUT YOUR HAIR while you're sleeping!

> I'm glad she left the Shore House, because I was about to Jerry Springer her ass.
> —Mike "The Situation"

IF YOU'RE THAT STUPID and you want to leave the Jersey Shore in the summertime, then I'm gonna let you leave. —Pauly D

ANGELINA'S THIS TYPICAL STATEN ISLAND GIRL. I know the way they talk. They get f*ckin' mad and they always want to point their f*ckin' fingers. And they get up, they cause a f*ckin' hissy fit and they turn into the f*ckin' biggest stupid bitches ever. —Vinnie

ANGELINA WAS LIKE A HALF-ASSED FIRECRACKER. IT JUST FIZZLED OUT REAL QUICK AND IT MADE A LOUD NOISE.

—MIKE "THE SITUATION"

THE FAMILY

IF YOU LEAVE, I'M GONNA STUFF YOUR F*CKIN' NOSE WITH TAMPONS.
—SNOOKI (TO JWOWW)

I WAS FEELING LIKE AN OUTCAST, but now I feel like I'm part of the family now. They're starting to get to know me. . . . They're like, "You know what, Snooki? You're a really cool girl." I'm like, "Thank you!" Like, "Finally!" —Snooki

I'M REALLY NOT JEALOUS OF SAM AND RONNIE because, I mean, I had my choice, okay, and it's really no sweat off my back 'cause she wanted me. —Mike "The Situation"

You stumpy bastard.
—Sammi

YOU'RE A STUMPY BASTARD, TOO. Listen, with your Flintstone big toe, with your doorstop big toe. —Ronnie

THE WHOLE RONNIE AND SAM SITUATION may be crumbling as we speak, it's only a matter of time before she's gonna pull the eject button. —Mike "The Situation"

I LIKE MY CLOTHES LIKE MY WOMEN . . . options. —Mike "The Situation"

YOU LIKE YOUR GIRLS like your underwear . . . dirty. —Vinny

LOOK AT THIS LITTLE CANDY SMILE HE'S GOT. Like he's about to meet my sister. See, he realizes how pretty I am and he wants to see my sister. —Mike "The Situation"

SHE'S MIKE WITHOUT A SIX-PACK . . . She looked like Mike with a wig on. I was a little bit freaked out. —Vinny

YOU HAVE NO GAME at all. —Mike "The Situation"

REALLY? That's not what your sister said. —Vinny

WE'RE AT THE BEACH, Mike's creeping on the first girl he sees, of course. The girl's, like, teenage area. —Vinny

SHE WAS EIGHTEEN. That ass did not look twelve.
—Mike "The Situation"

I DON'T NEED NO FAMILY MEETINGS.

I DON'T NEED TO TRUST IN SNICKERS.

I DON'T EVEN TRUST IN F*CKIN' JENNI.

—SAMMI

THE PRINCESS OF POUGHKEEPSIE

SNOOKI

MY BOOBS ARE SO TIGHT I CAN'T BREATHE. IS THAT NORMAL?

MY ULTIMATE DREAM IS TO MOVE TO JERSEY, find a nice juiced hot tanned guy and live my life.

SNOOKIN' FOR LOVE. Honestly, that's all I'm doing here: "Snookin' for love."

I DELIVERED A FRIGGIN' CALF FROM A COW!

I think my crotch is sticking out.

GUIDO APPLICATIONS over here!

F*CK MY LIFE. Seriously. F*ck my life.

I WAS WEARING MY CORSET, I look slutty, but I don't give a f*ck. I can wear whatever the f*ck I want.

I HAD A FEELING where I wanted to make out with somebody, so I just made out with Ryder, 'cause all the guys like that.

I THINK WHAT HAPPENED TO SNICKERS brought us a lot closer to Snickers. 'Cause now we like kinda feel bad and she's a real person. I mean, we get on her and stuff like that but we still care for her. —Pauly D

NOW I KNOW THAT THEY ALL LOVE ME LIKE I LOVE THEM. I stuck up for them—that's why I got hit in the face. And I think they realize that and they realize I'm a nice person and I care about everybody in this house. So now they all feel the same way about me. —Snooki

LIKE, VETERINARIAN, like, that's my soul. Like, I f*ckin' save animals, like, that's what I do. —Snooki

SNOOKI'S OUTFIT IS CRAZY, she looks like a birthday cake, she's all decorated, dressed up, with the pink, boobs all up in her face, I guess she wants to go out with a big bang, literally. —Vinny

END

IT TAKES A SPECIAL TYPE of a person to get through this. We all should be proud that we balled out and had an awesome time. —Mike "The Situation"

WE STAYED BOYS throughout this whole thing. This bond that we shared brings us together and no one can ever take that away from us, ever. Like, we take that with us for life, this bond . . . That was deep. —Pauly D

I DID GROW UP. I grew up a lot. And I survived here and I did it on my own. I think I've come a long way. I'm f*ckin' mature and I'm a better person. And it really changed me here. The Jersey Shore changed me. —Snooki

95

Compiled and Edited by Wenonah Doret
Photographs by Scott Gries
DVD Edited by Mark Hall; Produced by Eric Stringer

Special Thanks To: Allyssa Agro, Scott Birchman, Mark Breese, Walter Einenkel, Jackie French, Stacy Gee, Andrew Han, Jennifer Heddle, Jodi Lahaye, Chris Linn, Emilia Pisani, Andreea Radulescu, Rosanne Russo, Lisa Silfen, Lawrence Toscano, Shannon Toumey, Jessica Zalkind, Anthony Ziccardi

Gallery Books
A Division of Simon & Schuster, Inc.
1230 Avenue of the Americas, New York, NY 10020

First MTV Books/Gallery Books trade paperback edition June 2010

GALLERY BOOKS and colophon are registered trademarks of Simon & Schuster, Inc.

For information about special discounts for bulk purchases, please contact Simon & Schuster Special Sales at 1-866-506-1949 or business@simonandschuster.com

The Simon & Schuster Speakers Bureau can bring authors to your live event. For more information or to book an event contact the Simon & Schuster Speakers Bureau at 1-866-248-3049 or visit our website at www.simonspeakers.com.

Designed by Timothy Shaner, nightanddaydesign.biz

Manufactured in Mexico

1 3 5 7 9 10 8 6 4 2

Library of Congress Cataloging-in-Publication Data is available.

ISBN 978-1-4391-9682-3   ISBN 978-1-4391-9916-9 (ebook)